Second-Hand Coat

Second-Hand Coat

Coat

POEMS NEW AND SELECTED

Ruth Stone

Yellow Moon Press
CAMBRIDGE

Reprinted 1991
Yellow Moon Press
P. O. Box 1316
Cambridge, Massachusetts 02238
First published 1987 by David R. Godine, Publisher, Inc.

Some of the poems in Part I of this volume originally appeared
in *The American Poetry Review, The California Quarterly,
Choomia, Embers, Field, Feminist Studies, Footwork,
Greenhouse, The Iowa Review, Kentucky Poetry Review,
Ploughshares, Poets-On, River City Review.*

ISBN 0-938756-33-8

Also by Ruth Stone:

Who Is The Widow's Muse 1991 Yellow Moon Press

To
my brilliant enduring friends
Sandra Gilbert and Elliot Gilbert

For
Nora Swan Croll,
Ehsan Jessie Croll,
Ethan David Carlson,
Hillery Ruth Stone,
Bianca Rose Stone,
Walter Joseph Stone,
my dear grandchildren

and to
William B. Goodman,
editor and friend

Contents

III. *from* **Topography**

I

Second-Hand Coat

Second-Hand Coat

I feel
in her pockets; she wore nice cotton gloves,
kept a handkerchief box, washed her undies,
ate at the Holiday Inn, had a basement freezer,
belonged to a bridge club.
I think when I wake in the morning
that I have turned into her.
She hangs in the hall downstairs,
a shadow with pulled threads.
I slip her over my arms, skin of a matron.
Where are you? I say to myself, to the orphaned body,
and her coat says,
Get your purse, have you got your keys?

Where I Came From

My father put me in my mother
but he didn't pick me out.
I am my own quick woman.
What drew him to my mother?
Beating his drumsticks
he thought — why not?
And he gave her an umbrella.
Their marriage was like that.
She hid ironically in her apron.
Sometimes she cried into the biscuit dough.
When she wanted to make a point
she would sing a hymn or an old song.
He was loose-footed. He couldn't be counted on
until his pockets were empty.
When he was home the kettle drums,
the snare drum, the celeste,
the triangle throbbed.
While he changed their heads,
the drum skins soaked in the bathtub.
Collapsed and wrinkled, they floated
like huge used condoms.

At the Center

The center is simple, they say.
They say at the Fermi accelerator,
"Rejoice. A clear and clean
explanation of matter is possible,"
as they bombard subatomic particles
at energies never before attained.

Today it rained. Out in the orchard
linens that were slept in so hard
skin flaked between the threads
and animal odor mixed with the soapy steam,
the linens are washed and rinsed.
Wind comes up between the trees
snapping the sheets. Where is this place,
the center they speak of? Currants,
red as faraway suns, burn on the currant bush.
Your eyes, the eyes of a madman that I loved,
far underground, fall apart,
while their particles still shoot like meteors
through space making their own isolated trajectories.

Poetry

I sit with my cup
to catch the crazy falling alphabet.
It crashes, it gravels down,
a fault in the hemispheres.
High-rise *L*'s, without windows—
buckling in slow motion;
Subway *G*'s, *Y*'s, twisted,
collapsing underground:
screams of passengers
buried in the terrible phonemes,
arms and legs paralyzed.
And no one, no one at all,
is sifting through the rubble.

How to Catch Aunt Harriette

Mary Cassatt has her in a striped dress with a
child on her lap, the child's foot in a wash basin.
Or Charlotte Mew speaks in her voice of the feeling
that comes at evening with home-cawing rooks.
Or Aunt Harriette sometimes makes an ineffable
gesture between the lines of Trollope.
In Indianapolis, together we rode the belching city bus to
high school. It was my first year, she was a senior. We were
nauseated every day by the fumes, by the unbearable
streets. Aunt Harriette was the last issue of my
Victorian grandparents. Once after school she
invited me to go with her to Verner's.
What was *Verner's?* I didn't ask and Aunt Harriette didn't say.
We walked three miles down manicured Meridian.
My heels rubbed to soft blisters. Entering an empty
wood-echoing room fronting the sidewalk,
we sat at a plain plank table and Aunt Harriette
ordered two glasses of iced ginger ale.
The varnish of light on Aunt Harriette
had the quality of a small eighteenth-century
Dutch painting. My tongue with all its buds intact
slipped in the amber sting. It was my first hint
of the connoisseur, an induction rarely repeated;
yet so bizarre, so beyond me,
that I planned my entire life from its indications.

Scars

Sometimes I am on a train
going to a strange city,
and you are outside the window
explaining your suicide,
nagging me like a sick child.
I have no unbroken rest.
Sometimes I cover you
with an alphabet
or the steers bellow your name
asking the impossible of me.
The chicory flowers speak for you.
They stare at the sky
as though I am invisible.
Often the distance from
here to the pond changes.
Last night a green fire
came down like a space ship,
and I remembered
those people in Argentina
who went inside one
where it burnt the grass,
and forgot their measures
like clabbered milk,
forgot who they meant to be
or suspected they might become,
and later showed the scars
on their foreheads
to everyone,
begging them to believe.

What Can You Do?

Mrs. Dubosky pulls a handful
of sharpened pencils out of her apron pocket.
They're for the grandchildren.
She picks envelopes out of wastepaper baskets
and soaks off the stamps.
The boys have a stamp collection.
Mrs. Dubosky is paying on a trailer.
She can't retire until she's paid off the seven thousand.
She's sixty-two.
Mrs. Dubosky says, "We'll see."
Her new daughter-in-law lives in the trailer.
Her old daughter-in-law has the house.
"What are you going to do?" Mrs. Dubosky says,
looking at me. "He's my only son.
He'd come home. Want a kiss.
You know, those private things.
He's away all week pulling that semi to New Jersey.
And she says, 'Not now. I'm busy.'
Or, 'Leave me alone.'
He says, 'Ma, right then I knew.'
He made himself a bed upstairs.
He said, 'Let her go on, who cares?'
Then he asked her, 'How come Don is here
when I get home midnight? He's got a wife and kids.
What's he doing here all the time?' And she says,
'Are you accusing me?'
You know, I had my trailer on my son's land.
I had the hole under it for the flush toilet
and I had to move it to a trailer park.
That woman got everything."
Mrs. Dubosky wears other people's old tennis shoes.
Chemicals in the cleaning water eat right through them.
She's got a bad leg.
Her mother's legs were bad. They had to be amputated.
While her mother was in the hospital,

her father's colostomy quit working and he got a blockage.
Her mother told her, "You burnt him. I know you did."
"Oh, no, Ma."
"Yes, you did," she said. "I saw it in the paper."
"Marriage," says Mrs. Dubosky. "You know how it is.
I had just had the baby.
My husband was after me all the time.
You know, physical.
Oh, he slapped me but that's not what I mean.
My mother came over and she said,
'What's the matter with you?'
You know, the eyebags was down on the cheeks.
I says, 'He's always after me,'
and she says, 'You're gonna come home.'
The judge said he'd never seen a case that bad.
You know what he called him? He said,
'You're nothing but a beast.' "
Mrs. Dubosky isn't sure. She says,
"What can you do?"
When she retires, she tells me,
she's going to get a dog. One of those nice little ones.
"When you rub them on the belly
they lie back limp," she says, "and just let you."

Drought in the Lower Fields

Steers are dumb like angels,
moony-eyed, and soft-calling
like channel bells
to sound the abyss,
the drop-off in the fog
that crows circle
and gliding buzzards
yearn down into with their small
red heads bent
looking for dead souls to pick.
Steers nod their heads, yes,
browsing the scalded grass,
they eat around the scarce
blue stars of chicory.

Moving Right Along

At the molecular level,
in another dimension,
oy, are you different!
That's where it all shreds
like Watergate.
You feel out there
like a bag of Ping-Pong balls,
the ends of your fingers leaking
tiny balloons at a Republican rally,
everyone voting for what you
are most afraid they
will vote for.
You're the one with the trash bag
stooping between rows of seats
in an empty convention hall,
whispering, "What's this?"
and lying awake at night
reading *Prevention Magazine,*
your shelves filling up
with bottles of rancid vitamins,
rows of bottles stubborn as farmers
marching to Washington,
disturbing traffic, the police,
the Department of Agriculture,
where no one will meet with them,
where their John Deeres,
their harvesters,
recalling objects in the Smithsonian,
are helpless to stop
the grinding laws of entropy.

Pokeberries

I started out in the Virginia mountains
with my grandma's pansy bed
and my Aunt Maud's dandelion wine.
We lived on greens and back-fat and biscuits.
My Aunt Maud scrubbed right through the linoleum.
My daddy was a northerner who played drums
and chewed tobacco and gambled.
He married my mama on the rebound.
Who would want an ignorant hill girl with red hair?
They took a Pullman up to Indianapolis
and someone stole my daddy's wallet.
My whole life has been stained with pokeberries.
No man seemed right for me. I was awkward
until I found a good wood-burning stove.
There is no use asking what it means.
With my first piece of ready cash I bought my own
place in Vermont; kerosene lamps, dirt road.
I'm sticking here like a porcupine up a tree.
Like the one our neighbor shot. Its bones and skin
hung there for three years in the orchard.
No amount of knowledge can shake my grandma out of me;
or my Aunt Maud; or my mama, who didn't just bite an apple
with her big white teeth. She split it in two.

Mother's Picture

From a photograph on the bedroom wall,
you look toward what we cannot see.
The shadow of silver trembles
in its journey to nowhere.
You look past us without words,
a young woman we never knew.
When light comes in the room,
the uncompromising bed
does not translate your suffering.
You stare from inside the picture
wordless as the virgin oaks on Lake Kegonsa,
though they cry in the ice storms
with the voices of the waterfowl.
The wild swans cross over
that lake in late March.
Your look is silent as their shadows
flying on the reedy bottom.

Liebeslied

The landlord's child
cries at night
in the next room.
It is early winter
and bright
in the morning,
the leaves of the apricot
still firmly attached.

Out by the oleander
a female cat
who lives wild
among these tract houses
waits for the food
I have begun to put outside.
Sometimes two half-grown
kittens come with her.

I look at the folded plastic chairs
thrown carelessly down
on the cement patio,
the toy truck
stopped in its forward surge
just where it is
loaded with mildewed walnuts.

I remember my father
whistling late at night.
He is walking along Irvington Avenue
from the streetcar line.
Alone, downstairs
he winds up the phonograph —
at the wavering edge
Fritz Kreisler's *Liebeslied*.
I listen in the dark

to the bowed strings of sadness and pain
to what the human voice
beyond itself
is telling me.

Curtains

Putting up new curtains,
other windows intrude.
As though it is that first winter in Cambridge
when you and I had just moved in.
Now cold borscht alone in a bare kitchen.

What does it mean if I say this years later?

Listen, last night
I am on a crying jag
with my landlord, Mr. Tempesta.
I sneaked in two cats.
He screams NO PETS! NO PETS!
I become my Aunt Virginia,
proud but weak in the head.
I remember Anna Magnani.
I throw a few books. I shout.
He wipes his eyes and opens his hands.
OK OK keep the dirty animals
but no nails in the walls.
We cry together.
I am so nervous, he says.

I want to dig you up and say, look,
it's like the time, remember,
when I ran into our living room naked
to get rid of that fire inspector.

See what you miss by being dead?

Something

In a room upstairs, under the hot roof,
the infants long for something
as they tear up their books,
as they throw the pieces of Mr. Potato Head.

It is calm after the rain.
On the hill behind the house
the green pup-tent gapes open
beside the wading pool of white and red.
Marking a broken driveway,
asters fringe in the plain weeds.

The family has been fed.
The mother sits on the patio
having a cigarette.
It is getting dark.

In the grass around the house,
in the neighbors' yards,
along the edges of the roads,
as if at a signal, there begins
a subliminal rattle
and steady sifting fall of ripened seeds.

From the Arboretum

The bunya-bunya is a great louse that sucks.
From its center many limbs are fastened to the sky
which lies behind it placidly suffering.
At its bottom it wears the ruffles of a cancan girl.
Bird dung and nits drip with its resinous sweat.
Its forgotten threads underground are anaerobic
with the maximum strength of steel. For every stretch
upward it splits and bleeds — fingers grow out of fingers.
Rings of ants, bark beetles, sponge molds,
even cockroaches communicate in its armpits.
But it protests only with the voices of starlings,
their colony at its top in the forward brush.
To them it is only an old armchair, a brothel, the front porch.

Winter

The ten o'clock train to New York,
coaches like loaves of bread powdered with snow.
Steam wheezes between the couplings.
Stripped to plywood, the station's cement standing room
imitates a Russian novel. It is now that I remember you.
Your profile becomes the carved handle of a letter knife.
Your heavy-lidded eyes slip under the seal of my widowhood.
It is another raw winter. Stray cats are suffering.
Starlings crowd the edges of chimneys.
It is a drab misery that urges me to remember you.
I think about the subjugation of women and horses;
brutal exposure; weather that forces, that strips.
In our time we met in ornate stations
arching up with nineteenth-century optimism.
I remember you running beside the train waving good-bye.
I can produce a facsimile of you standing
behind a column of polished oak to surprise me.
Am I going toward you or away from you on this train?
Discarded junk of other minds is strewn beside the tracks:
mounds of rusting wire, grotesque pop art of dead motors,
senile warehouses. The train passes a station;
fresh people standing on the platform,
their faces expecting something.
I feel their entire histories ravish me.

Shadows

I receive a card that says you have a walled garden,
a pomegranate tree. You sometimes go to Shiraz.
You have thrown a blanket over your table.
Underneath there is a lamp to warm your feet.
The maid, Batool, works all day long for a few rials.
Her son takes her money.
Her husband divorced her with three words.
You send a color photograph
in which your shadow crosses a bed of flowers.
There is a garden pool, espaliered grapes,
an orange and blue striped awning over a terrace.
"Along the street," you say, "the men hold hands.
The women are covered with black chadors."
You have gone to the mountains to ski.
You are in love. You have lost twenty pounds.
You chain smoke. You miss me. You need money.

The letter lags a month behind.
Your shadow sways with a donkey
stippled on Carpathian grass.
The rippling plateau fades toward the mountains of Iran.

I search for you in flashing neurons.
Across wrinkled dunes beyond hearing,
pure random donkey bells, dry resonance;
rocks sliding against the stubborn pull.
Mauve patches on the donkey's underbelly,
worn to smooth leather. Slap of thongs.
Below, falling away like the eye of God,
the deep iris of the Caspian Sea.

The Miracle

Come to the window Aunt Bess said.
Uncle Ivan was down there among the sheets walking by.
The Ku Klux Klan was out protecting little girls.
I cried for my baby brother playing in the yard,
pulling him by his romper suit into the house,
while an old black man in a horse drawn wagon,
the reins slack in his hands,
passed slow — the hot road under the wheels
whispering dust and I'll get you little girl.
Purple bodies hung in my head.
Fiery crosses burned in my bed.
Aunt Bess talked about this. There was
so little to do in the summer,
Newport News so quiet you heard teaspoons
stirring the ice tea in glasses
on the vine shaded porches, the faint
protest of the porch swings,
the fret of the women's voices.

My mother worried about her sister,
her sister's marriage.
Aunt Bess was taking Lydia E. Pinkham's Vegetable Compound
and praying for conception.
Uncle Ivan was out, away; there was
quarreling, Aunt Bess lying by day in her room
with headaches, washcloths on her forehead,
her eyes in the morning red-rimmed.
The smell of chicory in the coffee,
fried apples, fried potatoes, corn bread,
she wanted nothing but a miracle
from the ghost with a business suit under his sheet,
his shoes dropping so late,
coming in whiskey-arrogant, from tarts,
from parlor chippies, Aunt Bess said.

That summer seeds grew deep, dark tendrils sprouted.
My mother and Aunt Bess bent over bits of cloth.
Little Ivan, my cousin, took me under the bed
with a promise of paper dolls, sheets falling around us.
I was five. I don't remember what he did.
We went home in the fall by ferry across the Elizabeth
River to Norfolk. My father had straightened
things out. The house and the wicker furniture
were all there. The fat boy next door was still fat.
Lightning still flashed even when I hid
in my closet. Next spring, it must have been spring,
my mother was telling my father it was Lydia E. Pinkham's
that did it, that little Audry came out of the bottle
of tonic. It was a miracle, that the baby had curls,
a full year's growth of hair and a perfect head.

A year later Uncle Ivan ran off, just disappeared.
Up to some flimflam with an Indian, according to Aunt Bess.
Little Audry was already rotten spoiled.
Then Little Ivan was killed out west in a stolen car.
We went to Newport News to sit with my aunt.
She was now a practical nurse in the hire of a woman
with cancer. We sat on the woman's couch.
The letter that came from the sheriff said
at the time they didn't know who Little Ivan was,
so they had gone to some expense and buried him.

I was in second grade when we moved up north.
My past faded, the South. I forgot about Little Ivan.
But when I turned thirteen I remembered
that he never gave me those paper dolls.
After all that fuss he was my only molester,
the dark body I was prepared for, the fiery cross
between my legs. And I began to keep him under my sheets;
I wore him out in the creases of my brain.
While he lay from his sixteenth year in a pauper's grave.

You May Ask

It is spring on the coast—
the sun behaving as it should
burning into the window
flashing against this poem.
This poem celebrates a fly
that softly rises above the desk.
Not arrogant, it thinks
where have I been? Where
am I now? What year is this?

Names

My grandmother's name was Nora Swan.
Old Aden Swan was her father. But who was her mother?
I don't know my great-grandmother's name.
I don't know how many children she bore.
Like rings of a tree the years of woman's fertility.
Who were my great-aunt Swans?
For every year a child; diphtheria, dropsy, typhoid.
Who can bother naming all those women churning butter,
leaning on scrub boards, holding to iron bedposts,
sweating in labor? My grandmother knew the names
of all the plants on the mountain. Those were the names
she spoke of to me. Sorrel, lamb's ear, spleenwort, heal-all;
never go hungry, she said, when you can gather a pot of greens.
She had a finely drawn head under a smooth cap of hair
pulled back to a bun. Her deep-set eyes were quick to notice
in love and anger. Who are the women who nurtured her for
      me?
Who handed her in swaddling flannel to my great-grandmother's
      breast?
Who are the women who brought my great-grandmother tea
and straightened her bed? As anemone in midsummer, the air
cannot find them and grandmother's been at rest for forty years.
In me are all the names I can remember—pennyroyal, boneset,
bedstraw, toadflax—from whom I did descend in perpetuity.

Why Kid Yourself

Snow, that white anesthesia, evaporates.
It's gone like a lover after the morning paper.
An entire mountain blushes.
Everything's been at it.
Embarrassing bodies are pushing out.
Plants, animals, swollen with excess
are straining to keep their balance.
Two hot days and the population explodes off the circuits,
jams the sewers.
Afterbirth reeks in the swamps, gluts the rivers.
And everything that lived through last year
is out fattening itself, eating the babies.

Message from Your Toes

Even in the absence of light
there is light. Even in the least electron
there are photons.
So in a larger sense you must consider your own toes.
Far from notice they spin
with their soft cheese-grains,
their ingrown nails;
your pink buds, identifying pads.
Down there the blood hurls
its collecting ooze of oxygen.
Down there the nerves thick as cables
in an ocean bed, collect barnacles;
clasped by octopods, send distant messages
years late, after the loved is gone,
the lips dead, after slugs have eaten
the remembered face. Relay how once
he stumbled across a room, breaking a bone,
a middle toe; how he suffered and couldn't wear shoes;
how his pain spoiled three months of summer.
How now, if you should dig him up, the bones of his left foot
falling like dice, there would be one among them gnarled out
    of shape,
a ridge of calcium extruding a pattern of unutterable anguish.
And your toes, passengers of the extreme
clustered on your dough-white body,
say how they miss his feet, the thin elegance of his ankles.

Sunday

The Masons spent Sundays visiting the hospital.
It was their weekly outing.
They liked to talk surgery.
Mrs. Mason's fat had been surgically removed.
Glen had had his appendix out.
The accident wing stirred up their blood.
The Masons lifted their hands in significant salutes
as they went by open doors.
They got high on ether. They were into sutures.
"Hi, doc." That's old doc Booferman, they'd say.
They talked about Helen Goochal's kidneys,
(doc was sweating her out).
The Masons liked to get into medical history.
Long antiseptic Sundays, tubes of interstitial fluids,
bed pans, strangers lying in metal beds.
They got off on face masks.
They liked to press their thumbs on your wrist
and feel your pulse.
During the week they talked cases with the pharmacist
at Buckville Drugs. But Sunday
after a heavy dinner, they'd get dressed
and one of them would say, "Well, what you wanta do?
Go to the hospital?"

Pine Cones

Flat against the sky
they are lice sucking.
The tree is infested with them.
Drought bleaches the needles.
Branches scab.
The tree is an old bum.
It's gone so long without water,
it's really repelled by water.
Its roots crawl after an osmotic fix with the sewer.

Pine cones
are hard brown rib cages;
barrel chested tiny proto-Homo-sapiens
exhumed from Olduvai Gorge;
missing links
between animal and vegetable.

Upended pine cones
are pagodas.
Inside each one,
with much ceremony,
honorable seeds consider
ancient balance:
fertility   futility.

Father's Day

When I was eight you put me
on the Sky-Line roller coaster at Riverside
where I screamed all day
holding to a steel bar
unable to get off.
While you were shaking dice behind a tent,
I was rising and falling,
a strip of tickets crumpled in my hand.
In 1950 you were reading Epictetus late at night
falling asleep in your chair.
Years earlier you wrote in your diary,
"New girl in town. Quinn and I
had a shot at her."
Sitting in the orchestra pit
drumming the pratfalls,
the vaudeville timed to your wrist rolls.
My first groom. Mother was shy.
She said I could not marry you.
She kept me for myself.
She did not know the wet lips
you kissed me with one morning.
What an irritable man you were.
Rising and falling,
I could not remember who I was.
Whole summers consumed
in the sound of glass wind-chimes.
When you died they scattered your ashes in a field.
At any moment I can breathe in the burned powder of
    your body,
the bitter taste, the residue.

Orange Poem Praising Brown

The quick brown poem jumped over the lazy woman.
There it goes flapping like an orange with peeling wings.
Like an old dried orange with hard peel wings.
The thick brown poem jumped over the desperate woman.
There you go my segments, my divided fruit, escaping.
The thick woman jumped over the lousy poem. It's Brown,
    she sighed.
Watch it, the poem cried. You aren't wearing any pants.
The empty places of the poem. The odor of the poem.
Brown approached. Praise my loose hung dangle, he said.
Tell me about myself in oral fragments.
Refer to Brown. Not you. Not her.
The thick lenses through which the poem lurks.
Come, says the poem, see my harmless teeth. Kiss my vicious
    lips.
Rising in the greasy air, the orange poem heavy with brown
goes to the dump. It does not even like the taste of itself.
The thick typewriter jumps over the lazy poet.
You have not yet praised Brown, it said, and you
call yourself a poet. Jump over that.

The Room

The room is the belly of the house.
It is pregnant with you.
It belches you out the door.
It sucks you in like a minnow.

You are a parasite in the room.
The room distorts with your ego.
It withholds itself from you.
It looks at you with criminal eyes.

Opinions insinuate from the baseboards.
The molding and ceiling are strange, erudite.
They see only the top of your head.
The floor, however, is continuously looking up your skirt.

The room keeps its weapons in a side pocket.
You should be hung in the closet, it says.
You should sweep up your hair, you are shedding.
You are spoiling my mattress.

Unable to hold your shape you dissolve in the room.
It fastens itself to your skin like a lamprey.
When you thrust yourself out the door,
it peels from your back and snaps like a rubber stocking.
It gathers itself in a corner and waits for you.

American Milk

Then the butter we put on our white bread
was colored with butter yellow, a cancerous dye,
and all the fourth grades were taken by streetcar
to the Dunky Company to see milk processed; milk bottles
riding on narrow metal cogs through little doors that flapped.
The sour damp smell of milky-wet cement floors:
we looked through great glass windows at the milk.
Before we were herded back to the streetcar line,
we were each given a half pint of milk in tiny
milk bottles with straws to suck it up. In this way
we gradually learned about our country.

How Aunt Maud
Took to Being a Woman

A long hill sloped down to Aunt Maud's brick house.
You could climb an open stairway up the back
to a plank landing where she kept her crocks of wine.
I got sick on stolen angelfood cake and green wine
and slept in her feather bed for a week.
Nobody said a word. Aunt Maud just shifted
the bottles. Aunt's closets were all cedar lined.
She used the same pattern for her house dresses —
thirty years. Plain ugly, closets full of them,
you could generally find a new one cut and laid
out on her sewing machine. She preserved,
she canned. Her jars climbed the basement walls.
She was a vengeful housekeeper. She kept the blinds
pulled down in the parlor. Nobody really walked
on her hardwood floors. You lived in the kitchen.
Uncle Cal spent a lot of time on the back porch
waiting to be let in.

Comments of the Mild

The cabinet squats trembling on its carved legs,
an essence of trappings. Inside on the awkward shelves,
a cast-off bedspread, two stolen books.
From no period at all; in fact, the back legs are not carved,
while the front ones have turned balls. It tries to be Spanish,
Louis Quinze, Sheraton, Hilton Plaza. It is a bastard
from a tract house. There was no cabinetmaker.
It grew with a lot who were cut on band saws,
glued together on an assembly line, and stained
in a warehouse. "I am furniture," it says, in a subdued voice.
Not useful, not even ornamental, it has a certain bulk presence.
It takes the place of those who are not with you.
When you wake in the night, you sense that you are not alone.
There is someone else. But you forget who it is.
Sometimes passing the cabinet, you open the part that looks
like the confessional box. It is stern and empty.
Nothing fits in there, not even your head.

An Academic Life

The philosopher's red-haired voice
was like sawdust.
He suffered from asthma.
That is, he wore a trench coat
and once put his fist through a wall.
His wife's mother, after her last operation,
trotted down the hallway of his house
several times a night
with her tube and plastic bottle,
glad to be dying so happy,
and never once thought of the state of Washington
where her brand-new refrigerator
stood for five years covered with an old quilt
waiting in the yard for the electricity
to come, for the kitchen to be built.
His own split-level; he finally published,
was retained, a screw-in-plywood-assistant-professor.
He was the father of two boys
who tampered with parthenogenesis in frogs.
When he remembered them, between Carnap and Plato,
his eyes would fog, his neck would swell.

Procedure

Here is old Bessie laid out on a metal slab
ready for the cutting room.
Here goes her roller coaster on rubber wheels,
one at the head pushing it off, one guiding.
Doorways wink like thoughtful shoppers in the market
picking a weekend roast.

Here she is squeezed, knees up, back curled,
tight in the arms of the anesthetist.
He whispers her down into her spinal cord.
"Lord, I can't feel my feet," she says
meaning to get off the board
and get out of the butcher shop.

Here goes old Bessie chop for chop
and loin for loin, all her grits and greens
turned into tasty cuts. The surgeon loves her belly
like a razor loves a razor strop.
He peels her like potato skins,
dropping her middlings in a red trough.

Here goes old Bessie stitched with nylon thread,
rolling back on a platter
to vomit morphine,
threatening to wet her bed.
Here come two nurses with impassive faces
preparing another needle.

Here comes the surgeon wearing his sports jacket,
stopping to pat her hips. He pulls
the dividing curtain with a tremendous rustle.
More blood, more suspect tissue,
more fat, more gristle. His teeth are sharp.
He runs his expert finger over her uncut places.

When the Furnace Goes on in a California Tract House

If the blower is on
you may experience otherness —
then on the vinyl table
the clear plastic saltshaker
with her wide bottom, sexy waist,
and green plastic head,
her inner slope of free-running crystals,
is visibly crumbling
in the sight of the frankly opaque pepper
who seems taller, even threatening,
though they are the same size,
in fact, a designed pair.
His contents are hotter.
"Yes," she sighs, "the pepper is strong.
How he asserts himself on the cream soup — "
Or, "What is an egg without his gesture?"
Little does she suspect in her ability to dissolve
without losing herself, that the very blood . . .
"It's degrading," she confides, "the way they pinch me."

Icons from Indianapolis

The fountain around the soldiers' and sailors' monument,
the mist from the splashing water, the Murat Theater;
it was there I waited for the young man I loved,
hour after hour. Often he would not come.
I leaned against the walls of a candy shop,
boxes of rubber chocolates in the window,
behind me buses snoring their pneumatic doors.
His thin bent-down body too tall
like the priest he went away to be but never was;
often exhausting even my compulsion to wait for him.
Once when he kissed me I swooned. His name was
   Mike Tarpey.
Even after I was engaged to someone else,
I would meet him in the park. I was not Irish. I would walk
past Our Lady of Lourdes, the sisters starched into archways
beyond the cement Pietà. I doubted even the Presbyterians.
I could see the older black woman in the bus station,
pus running down her legs, gushing out of her,
the policeman coming to take her away. What were hats
and fur shawls when I knew that? She never left me.
From that time I carried her like an icon.
In these catacombs also he lies in perfect condition;
age nineteen, black hair, his thin jaw slightly out of line.
Was it that Picasso-like shift in planes that I could never
look at enough? These go with me where I go.
I wrap them in linens without prayers. I carry them.

Snow Trivia

In secret molecules
snow is going back into the sky.
From edge to edge
the glacier pauses; midwinter thaw.

Snow is more air than water.
Buried alive under its crystals
you might live for days.

One year in Vermont
sheep herders froze in July
during a freak snowstorm.

Road commissioners, intercoms,
snowplows at three a.m.
booming like Civil War cannons.
On the ski trails
wax and more wax. Pole uphill.
Ski racks on compacts,
front wheel drive.

When the airport in Tehran
imploded under four feet of snow,
a survivor said she felt only
a cold tremor before the roof came down.

The study of snowflakes can
be an interdepartmental discipline.

Before pollution, mothers created
ice cream by adding sugar and vanilla
to fresh snow.

Snow is deceptive.
Even in Nepal where the Abominable is,
the doomed climbers trapped
on a narrow ledge
which helicopters could not reach,
continued to be seen waving
and lighting flares
against the mountain until
they were blotted out
by snowfall.

The Latest Hotel Guest Walks Over Particles that Revolve in Seven Other Dimensions Controlling Latticed Space

It is an old established hotel.
She is here for two weeks.
Sitting in the room
toward the end of October,
she turns on three lamps
each with a sixty watt bulb.
The only window opens
on a dark funnel of brick and cement.
Tiny flakes of paint glitter
between the hairs on her arms.
Paint disintegrates from a ceiling
that has surely looked down on the bed beneath it
during World War Two,
the Korean War, Vietnam,
the Cuban crisis, little difficulties
with the Shah, covert action, and presently,
projected Star Wars.
In fact, within that time,
this home away from home, room 404,
probably now contains the escaped molecules,
radiation photons and particulate particles
of the hair and skin of all its former guests.
It would be a kind of queeze mixture of body fluids
and polyester fibers which if assembled,
might be sculptured into an android,
even programmed to weep and beat its head
and shout, "Which war? . . . How much?"
She feels its presence in the dim artificial light.
It is standing in the closet.
There is an obsolete rifle, a bayonet.
It is an antihero composed of all the lost neutrinos.
Its feet are bandaged with the lint of old sheets.

It is the rubbish of all the bodies who sweated here.
She hears it among her blouses and slacks
and she knows at this moment it is, at last,
counting from ten to zero.

Years Later

Years later my eyes clear up
and the blood veil turns into a net.
Through hexagonal holes, sections
of your arms appear, or the fingers
of your right hand, our innocent obsessions,
your eyebrows, individual hair follicles,
or the Mongol pockets of fat
along your high arrogant cheeks.
These parts of you are clear
and reasonable and finally tell me
that it is your skeleton I crave;
the way the bones of your feet,
fitted like the wing sockets of angels,
came toward me in time over the long
plateaus of ice; their delicate mouselike tread
printed in tracks of snow over my mind.

Surviving in Earlysville
with a Broken Window

Mr. Garvey tells me old window glass is frail.
A man dealing in cattle has use of his fields, steers graze
    his worn out acres.
He lives in Charlottesville, receives my rent by mail.

He's in heating and plumbing. He acquired this property
    at a delinquent taxes sale.
A scrubby graveyard in the pasture, enclosed with clay and
    quartz walls, designates some earlier forsakers.
Mr. Garvey tells me old window glass is frail.

It rains on the metal roof. The young steers bellow. My pale
sticky letters are all bills that come late in the afternoon
    from moneymakers.
And if the university doesn't screw up, he receives my rent
    by mail.

I'm vegetarian, talk to the steers. I say we must love each
    other and the great blue whale
and the gone silly dodo who helpfully scored in its
    gizzard the thick endocarps of the, for all purposes now,
    extinct calvaria tree; coevolution of seed and seed breaker.
Mr. Garvey, who never fixes anything, tells me old window
    glass is frail.

The graveyard has headstones with names and weathered head-
    and footstones without names. I inhale
a sourmash smell of fallen pears hollowed out by bees,
    those indigenous sweet-rakers.
The cattle dealer is starving the cattle while Mr. Garvey
    receives my rent by mail.

The house inside has wooden walls; is simple, spare, even
  severe; handhewn board, each nail
hand cut, driven across the grain. It's drafty, hard to
  heat in winter, and remains an anachronism to the easy takers.
The steers cross the dry stubble like wound up toys. They
  come to the fence at night and wait. Mr. Garvey tells me
  old window glass is frail.
He lives in Charlottesville, receives my rent by mail.

Turning

The habit of you lying next to me
was so strong that for a year
I slept with pillows on your side of the bed.

When I turned in my sleep
I put my arms around them
or as I often had before,
I turned away with my back against them —
this habit of tides waxing and waning.

Slowly during the years
the blood subsided.
When I dreamed of you,
you were standing with your back to me
facing the ocean, flat as a shadow
that cannot turn of itself.
A narrow strip separated rocky cliffs
of land from sea; under us, the shudder of sand,
enormous breakers eroding groins and jetties.

Happiness

We were married near the base,
with three days' leave;
a wife's allotment, a widow's pension.
The first night in our rented basement room,
as we came together . . .
Port Chicago exploded!
Several thousand pounds of human flesh
shot like hamburger through the air;
making military funerals, even with wax,
even with closed caskets, bizarre.
As well as certain facts:
there were no white males
loading ammunition on that ship.
From twenty miles away
shock waves rattled the roof,
the walls, the windows.
Our bed danced on the floor
as if we had created a miracle.

Then you went with your unit
in a leaky Liberty Ship to Kiska.
There in the shadow of a Russian church,
you began to notice birds.
One day you followed a snowbird over the tundra.
You followed it beyond sight of the camp, of the others,
as if for a moment there was a choice.
You felt a kind of happiness.
Your letters which told me this, with certain lines
removed, stamped out, sealed by the censor,
have been lost for years.
As the bird, filaments burning in a web of moss,
its tiny skeleton, its skull
that searched ahead of you like radar.

Turn Your Eyes Away

The gendarme came
to tell me you had hung yourself
on the door of a rented room
like an overcoat
like a bathrobe
hung from a hook;
when they forced the door open
your feet pushed against the floor.
Inside your skull
there was no room for us,
your circuits forgot me.
Even in Paris where we never were
I wait for you
knowing you will not come.
I remember your eyes as if I were
someone you had never seen,
a slight frown between your brows
considering me.
How could I have guessed
the plain-spoken stranger in your face,
your body, tagged in a drawer,
attached to nothing, incurious.
My sister, my spouse, you said,
in a place on the other side of the earth
where we lay in a single bed
unable to pull apart
breathing into each other,
the Gideon Bible open to the Song of Songs,
the rush of the El-train
jarring the window.
As if needles were stuck
in the pleasure zones of our brains,
we repeated everything
over and over and over.

Body Among Trees

Attached to trunks, mimicking shadows
lie on snow that evaporates.
Brush of nothing painting nothing.
It is not real. It is not you
walking in this woods. Every tree
listens to the sounds of the chain saw.
Not yet in the sweet meal of this year's rot,
the body walks by itself. The ground squirrel talks.
It is the air that receives, that is the translator.
Down the road, shoats frisk in nursery pens.
Neighbors conspire and grunt in breathy slops.
Up through ferocious loam, suffocating ferns,
every tree lashed its way to the light.
You say this to the body to comfort it.
It cannot be comforted. The chain saw cuts
liver, intestines, xylem, phloem — decapitates.
Arms are lopped. Something is dragged away.
You say to the body: it does not feel,
you must not grieve like this. It is not real.
You must not think it is real.

Some Things You'll Need to Know Before You Join the Union

I

At the poetry factory
body poems are writhing and bleeding.
An angry mob of women
is lined up at the back door
hoping for jobs.
Today at the poetry factory
they are driving needles through the poems.
Everyone's excited.
Mr. Po-Biz himself comes in from the front office.
He clenches his teeth.
"Anymore wildcat aborting out there," he hisses
"and you're all blacklisted."
The mob jeers.

II

The antiwar and human rights poems
are processed in the white room.
Everyone in there wears sterile gauze.
These poems go for a lot.
No one wants to mess up.
There's expensive equipment involved,
The workers have to be heavy,
very heavy.
These poems are packaged in cement.
You frequently hear them drop with a dull thud.

III

Poems are being shipped out
by freight car.
Headed up the ramp
they can't turn back.

49

They push each other along.
They will go to the packing houses.
The slaughter will be terrible,
an inevitable end of overproduction,
the poetry factory's GNP.
Their shelf life will be brief.

IV

They're stuffing at the poetry factory today.
They're jamming in images
saturated with *as* and *like*.
Lines are being stuffed to their limits.
If a line by chance explodes,
there's a great cheer.
However, most of them don't explode.
Most of them lie down and groan.

V

In the poetry factory
it's very hot.
The bellows are going,
the pressure is building up.
Young poems are being rolled out
ready to be cut.
Whistles are blowing.
Jive is rocking.
Barrels of thin words line the walls.
Fat words like links of sausages
hang on belts.
Floor walkers and straw bosses
take a coffee break.
Only the nervous apprentice
is anywhere near the machines

when a large poem
seems about to come off the assembly line.
"This is it," the apprentice shouts.
"Get my promotion ready!
APR, the quarterlies,
a chapbook, NEA,
a creative writing chair,
the poetry circuit, Yaddo!"
Inside the ambulance
as it drives away
he is still shouting,
"I'll grow a beard,
become an alcoholic,
consider suicide."

Women Laughing

Laughter from women gathers like reeds in the river.
A silence of light below their rhythm glazes the water.
They are on a rim of silence looking into the river.
Their laughter traces the water as kingfishers dipping
circles within circles set the reeds clicking;
and an upward rush of herons lifts out of the nests of laughter,
their long stick-legs dangling, herons, rising out of the river.

Translations

Forty-five years ago, Alexander Mehielovitch Touritzen,
son of a white Russian owner of a silk stocking factory
in Constantinople, we rumpled your rooming-house bed,
sneaked past your landlady and turned your plaster Madonna
to the wall. Are you out there short vulgar civil-engineer?
Did you know I left you for a Princeton geologist who called me
girlie? Ten years later he was still in the midwest when he died
under a rock fall. I told you I was pregnant. You gave me money
for the abortion. I lied to you. I needed clothes to go out with
the geologist. You called me *Kouschka*, little cat. Sometimes I
stopped by the civil-engineering library where you sat with other
foreign students. You were embarrassed; my husband might
catch you. He was in the chemistry lab with his Bunsen burner
boiling water for tea. Alexander Mehielovitch Touritzen, fig of
my pallid college days, plum of my head, did the silk stocking
factory go up in flames? Did the German fox jump out of the
desert's sleeve and gobble your father up? Are you dead?

Second-hand engine, formula concrete, we were still meeting in
stairwells when the best chess player in Champaign-Urbana went
to the Spanish Civil War. He couldn't resist heroic gestures. For
years I was haunted by the woman who smashed her starving
infant against the Spanish wall. Cautious, staid Mehielovitch, so
quick to pick my hairpins out of your bed.
Average lover, have your balls decayed?

Mehielovitch, my husband the chemist with light eyes and big
head, the one whose body I hated, came back in the flesh fifteen
years ago. He was wearing a tight western shirt he had made
himself. (There wasn't anything he couldn't do.) He talked about
wine- and cheese-tasting parties.
We folk danced at a ski lodge. So this is life, I said.
He told my daughter he was her daddy. It wasn't true.
You are all so boring. My friend from Japan, Cana Maeda, the

scholar of classical haiku, whose fingers, whose entire body had been trained to comply: her face pale without powder, her neck so easily bent, after she died from the radiation her translations of Bashō were published by interested men who failed to print her correct name. So the narrow book appears to have been written by a man. Faded in these ways, she is burned on my flesh as kimonos were burned on the flesh of women in the gamma rays of Hiroshima. She wasn't one of those whose skin peeled in the holocaust, whose bones cracked. Graceful and obscure, she was among all those others who died later. Where are you my repulsive white Russian? Are you also lost?

Pimpled obscene boy employed at an early age by your father, you pandered his merchandise on trays using your arm as a woman's leg slipped inside a silk stocking with a woman's shoe on your hand. Do you understand that later I lived with a transvestite, a hairdresser who wore wigs? When he felt that way he would go out and pick up an English professor. After we quarreled, I cut up his foam-rubber falsies. I had a garage sale while he was out of town. I sold his mail-order high heels, his corsets, his sequined evening gowns.

Those afternoons in bed listening to your memories of prostitutes with big breasts, how you wanted to roll on a mattress of mammary glands; the same when Rip Hanson told me about the invasion of France. Crossing the channel he saw infantry, falling past him from split open cargo planes, still clinging to tanks and bulldozers. Statistical losses figured in advance. The ripped-open remnants of a Russian girl nailed up by the Germans outside her village, also ancient, indigenous.
But what can I tell you about death? Even your sainted mother's
    soft dough body: her flour dusted breasts
by now are slime paths of microorganisms.
Where were you when they fed the multitudes to the ovens?

Old fetid fisheyes, did they roll you in at the cannery?
Did you build their bridges or blow them up?
Are you burned to powder? Were you mortarized?
Did you die in a ditch, Mehielovitch? Are you exorcised?

Poor innocent lecher, you believed in sin.
I see you rising with the angels, thin forgotten dirty-fingered son
of a silk stocking factory owner in Constantinople,
may you be exonerated. May you be forgiven.
May you be a wax taper in paradise,
Alexander Mehielovitch Touritzen.

A Last Cloud

Under the ozone the remnant swims
like an enormous fish.
Its shadow slides over the deserts.
Its milk flesh a new complex deadly crystal.
Its flat body a dust cloth of dry tears.
There is the old light, patient, bending.
There are the fragments of stars
still flying apart,
even the petals of galaxies,
the ion flowers.
Indifferent to the red earth,
the turning cinder crust, the burned exploding
rubble, the rotting waters —
above, the remnant moves,
solitary as your thought once was.

II

Cheap

Cheap

Not knowing I wasn't free
I would slam the door
Of his rented hacienda.
He was young and cheap;
Sweet smelling sweat.
I was easy in my sleep;
Gathered my hair
In a simple plait;
Not fretting myself.
And surely as sun up
He would follow me
From century plant
To lemon tree,
Over succulents and thorns,
Down to the stretching sand,
To the naked hiss,
Where he'd catch my hand
And we'd run blind as moles
With supple skins
Rubbing together like skeins
Of trader's silk;
Braying, galloping
Like a pair of mules.

Codicil

I am still bitter about the last place we stayed.
The bed was really too small for both of us.
In that same rooming house
Walls were lined with filing cases,
Drawers of birds' eggs packed in cotton.
The landlady described them.
As widow of the ornithologist,
Actually he was a postal clerk,
She was proprietor of the remains.
Had accompanied him on his holidays
Collecting eggs. Yes,
He would send her up the tree
And when she faltered he would shout,
"Put it in your mouth. Put it in your mouth."
It was nasty, she said,
Closing a drawer with her knee.
Faintly blue, freckled, mauve, taupe,
Chalk white eggs.
As we turned the second flight of stairs
Toward a mattress unfit for two,
Her voice would echo up the well,
Something about an electric kettle
At the foot of our bed.
Eggs, eggs, eggs in secret muted shapes in my head;
Hundreds of unborn wizened eggs.
I think about them when I think of you.

Loss

I hid sometimes in the closet among my own clothes.
It was no use. The pain would wake me
Or like a needle it would stitch its way into my dreams.
Wherever I turned
I saw its eyes looking out of the eyes of strangers.
In the night I would walk from room to room slowly
Like an old person in a convalescent home.
I would stare at the cornices, the dull arrangements of furniture.
It all remained the same.
It was not even a painting.
It was objects in space without any aura. No meaning attached.
Their very existence was a burden to me.
And I would go back to my bed whimpering.

From the Other Side

Maurice, had I known about salvation in art,
Child of pleasure, the affirmative,
While I swung from the monkey tree,
Would you have loved me more or less?
My metaphor, my suspect,
In pale recollection, apart from the elegance of your feet,
The truths of suffering return to me.

Gesture of open palms;
Your hands; your long fingers
Which were like rain on the western slopes.
I am disguised and travel with strangers.
I had no proofs of endings or beginnings.
In my simple animal,
Sleeping and waking were familiars of birth and death.
To wrap myself in your bony arms
Was the revelation of mortality.

Maurice, I seek salvation that is not there.
The measure of suffering is the knowledge of pleasure.
Consider the infinite anguish of this insanity;
Only in the impossible are we transformed to artifact.

The Tree

I was a child when you married me,
A child I was when I married you.
But I was a regular midwest child,
And you were a Jew.

My mother needled my father cold,
My father gambled his weekly gold,
And I stayed young in my mind, though old,
As your regular children do.

I didn't rah and I hardly raved.
I loved my pa while my mother slaved,
And it rubbed me raw how she scrimped and saved
When I was so new.

Then you took me in with your bony knees,
And it wasn't them that I wanted to please—
It was Jesus Christ that I had to squeeze;
Oh, glorious you.

Life in the dead sprang up in me,
I walked the waves of the salty sea,
I wept for my mother in Galilee,
My ardent Jew.

Love and touch and unity.
Parting and joining; the trinity
Was flesh, the mind and the will to be.
The world grew through me like a tree.

Flesh was the citadel but Rome
Was right as rain. From my humble home
I walked to the scaffold of pain, and the dome
Of heaven wept for her sensual son
Whom the Romans slew.

Was it I who was old when you hung, my Jew?
I shuffled and snuffled and whined for you.
And the child climbed up where the dead tree grew
And slowly died while she wept for you.

Goyim wept for the beautiful Jew.

Habit

Every day I dig you up
And wipe off the rime
And look at you.
You are my joke,
My poem.
Your eyelids pull back from their sockets.
Your mouth mildews in scallops.
Worm filaments sprout from the pockets
Of your good suit.
I hold your sleeves in my arms;
Your waist drops a little putrid flesh.
I show you my old shy breasts.

Illinois

Close up, shaved hay fields,
Corn stubble.
The horizon spins out flat.
Aluminum silo blinking in the sun.
Birds and gnats
Funnel up
Shading into tornados
Dancing along the edge of nowhere.
At your feet
Awkward sprays of chicory,
Blooming late;
Blue as imagined spaces,
Blue as a young pig's eyes.

Fading

As though approaching a mirror,
The post office recedes
To an unreal building in my mind.
I climb the public steps,
My former lightness inside clothes
Amazed at itself.
On the same shelf similar letters
Edged red and blue.
Encephalograms of difficult birth,
Butchered umbilical cords.
The same gray postal clerk
Moving more slowly by the minute.
The same squat provincial town
Dividing in hunks of cement.
I mail no letter to you,
Send no cry through the air
To fade out of time
As bending light.

U of My

When my dog barks and we go for a walk
I say to him, "avuncular, attaché, Williamsburg!"
And he pees on the evergreens.
"Horseradish," my cat cries after dark,
"Out, out." It is the fault
Of the university, of course,
That we live over the drying rooms;
That the laundry machines belch all night.
Recently an entire population of ants
Crept out of the geraniums
And is climbing the plaster.
Soon, I think, they will starve to death
Like those unfortunate people living
On lateritic soils, for these walls
Will not give up any nutrients.
I speak for them, "help, help!
Gestalt, Gestalt! University!
University of my dreams."

Dream of Wild Birds

Sweat curls off the lake the color of ochre.
The lead flamingo leaps flapping and dancing,
His neck contorted. He clicks his beak.
The water becomes blue-green. The sun rises.
This is a movie, a film, a picture, a little frame.
His bones, bathed in bird's blood, shine through
The x ray. His is an elegant skeleton.
His feathers, like the clouds, outlined with light,
Spreading, shaking. The wind coming in a thick current
Pulling loose down from his breast and whirling it
Up, up. It is a passion of light.
At once in slow motion the entire flock
Dances in pink ballet tutu, awkward grace, up and down,
Bowing and clicking. Meanwhile, the ovum is swelling
And the sperm is growing agitated. The time for leaving
The dark blood has come and the flagella lash against
The hot walls. The sun and the gnats burn over the lake
Catching fire in the feathers of the flamingos,
And the sun rises higher and higher.

Vegetables I

In the vegetable department
The eggplants lay in bruised disorder;
Gleaming, almost black,
Their skins oiled and bitter;
A mutilated stem twisting
From each swollen purple body
Where it had hung pendulous
From the parent.
They were almost the size
Of human heads, decapitated.
A fingernail tearing the skin
Disclosed pith, green white,
Utterly drained of blood.
Inside each skull, pulp;
Close packed, dry, and coarse.
As though the fontanels
Had ossified too soon.
Some of these seemed to be smiling
In a shy embarrassed manner,
Jostling among themselves.

Vegetables II

Saturated in the room
The ravaged curry and white wine
Tilt on the sink.
Tomatoes in plastic bag
Send up odors of resentment,
Rotting quietly.
It is the cutting room, the kitchen,
Where I go like an addict
To eat of death.
The eggplant is silent.
We put our heads together.
You are so smooth and cool and purple,
I say. Which of us will it be?

Periphery

You are not wanted
I said to the older body
Who was listening near the cupboards.
But outside on the porch
They were all eating.
The body dared not
Put its fingers in its mouth.
Behave, I whispered,
You have a wart on your cheek
And everyone knows you drink.
But that's all right, I relented,
It isn't generally known
How clever you are.
I know you aren't appreciated.
The body hunted for something good to eat,
But the food had all been eaten by the others.
They laughed together carelessly outside the kitchen.
The body hid in the pantry near the refrigerator.
After a while it laughed, too.
It listened to all the jokes and it laughed.

Separate

I want to tell you something with my hands.
I have been weeding the garden.
Many young people come here
Playing drums, picking strings,
Holding their wooden hearts.
The radishes are strong and pithy;
The lettuce is bolting.
The leaves of the radishes are jagged like knives.
These young people encamp around their instruments
As though they are around a fire.
They watch for the signal.
It passes between them.
Sometimes I water the toads
Who wait for insects under the zucchini leaves.
Indian bedspreads are not as gorgeous
As the muted patterns of toads.
Sometimes I lift a green lacewing
Out of a trough of water
And it stretches up like a cloud
Filling the universe with a gauze torque.
I want to tell you something with my fingers.
The space between us is a crack in the ice
Where light filters green to blue
Deeper than the fissures of continents.
All of time stretched like a web between
Was sucked into that space.
I want to tell you something with my hands,
My enormous hands which lie across a broken mirror
Reflected in broken pieces of themselves.

Overlapping Edges

Starlings flock to roost across rubble of shocked corn,
Last summer's scattered bone stalks ready to be ploughed
     under;
As though we were dismembered, as though we were in an
     open grave.
A veil of powdered limestone is suspended.
It is the fertilizer man in the corn field.
In the open pits of Auschwitz, scattered thigh bones, matchstick
     arms.
Through veils of limestone at the far edge,
Tombs of highrise apartments, silent, without lament.
And starlings, generations of birds puzzling along the windrows.

Communion

Birds circle above the hay barn.
A young bull gets up from the mud;
The tuft under his belly like a clump of grass.
He bellows; his curly throat stretched up,
His head half turned yearning upward from the wood slatted pen
Where he sleeps or tramples the sloughed manure.
The birds gather to cheep in unison.
A row of oak trees shining like waxed veneer
Ranges down windbreak.
The sky, vague blue behind a gauzy cumulus;
Pale fall sunlight glazes the barn shingles.
Now a chorus of bulls forcing music out of their bodies,
Begins and begins in terrible earnestness.
And the birds, undulating and rising, circle
And scatter over the fall ploughed strips.
What they are saying is out of their separateness.
This is the way it is. This is the way it is.

And Yet

Today feels like forever, and yet,
The gold striped wasp seems lean and overworked;
A backwoods mother with her wood not in
And the kerosene can almost empty.
She crawls over the split logs this way, that way.
She is distracted. But how still the leaves lie,
Drooping with inertia. The thick green has drained away.
Transparent now, red and yellow, they lie
On the air, languid, ready to let go. And yet,
The chickadee works his throat in the red pines,
Insisting on territory and a background of insects
Sings to fertility the hum of everlasting hope.
Here in the center of the forest the hot sun
Comes into the clearing. Soon it will snow.

Being a Woman

You can talk to yourself all you want to.
After all, you were the only one who ever heard
What you were saying. And even you forgot
Those brilliant flashes seen from afar, like Toledo
Brooding, burning up from the Moorish scimitar.

Sunk in umber, illuminated at the edges by fitful lightning,
You subside in the suburbs. Hidden in the shadow of hedges
You urge your dog to lift his leg on the neighbor's shrubs.

Soldiers are approaching. They are everywhere.
Behind the lamp-post the dog sends unknown messages
To the unknown. A sensible union of the senses.
The disengaged ego making its own patterns.
The voice of the urine saying this has washed away my salt,
My minerals. My kidneys bless you, defy you, invite you
To come out and yip with me in the schizophrenic night.

Cocks and Mares

Every man wants to be a stud.
His nature drives him.
Hanging between his legs
The heavy weight of scrotum.
He wants to bring forth God.
He wants God to come
Out of those common eggs.
But he can't tell his cock
From a rooster's. However,
I'm a horse, he says,
Prancing up and down.
What am I doing here
In the hen house?
Diddle you. Doodle doo.
In this fashion he goes on
Pretending that women are fowl
And that he is a stallion.
You can hear him crowing
When the wild mares
Come up out of the night fields
Whistling through their nostrils
In their rhythmic pounding,
In the sound of their deep breathing.

Shotgun Wedding

The bride is not yet married to the groom.
Caught in the last pose of a matron's dream,
She is a father's nightmare of illusion.
Trailing ribbons of gauzy particles,
The bridegroom's chariot
Exhorts the maidenly throngs
In fireworks, explosions!
They approach the zenith
Rowing the air like a pair of swans
With blood-red eyes.
In snowy plumage, restive,
With folded wings,
They tender themselves, ready to leap
And spread their fans to the showy entrances.
The musical anguish and anti-joy
Rumble in earth like thunder of fissures,
Warning too late
Of the descent
Into the anxious fingers and mouths
Of the hungry tribe.

Family

We left, repeating, "love . . . care."
The heaviness of bodies close;
Imbalance.
You were waiting until we were gone
To put back the records;
Vacuum.
We ate too much food;
Drank coffee, tea, beer.
It was difficult to fit
Into the uncomfortable chairs;
To sit waiting for something
To come to pass. Doorways
Were not in our heads.
We were too heavy to be inside
Denting and sagging the calendar.
You brought in the corpse to show
Its bloody stumps,
And killed it again out of boredom.
It stared without any memory,
Without arms or face.
It was all we had to kiss good-bye.

Mine

Sick at heart
I lie down
Among those who dream of murder.
While I am sleeping
They take away my blankets.
The sparrows fly up from the snow
And hunch in the bushes.
I walk slowly away, shivering.
I have died ahead of my body.
It drags behind me.
Come, they say, hiding their smiles,
Surely you can do something
About this bloody thing that is following you.
You know it is yours.

The Infant

The sky is a fat belly
Blown up with gas,
With millions of belly buttons.

The sky is a head turned away,
With long gray hairs.
It is looking at God.

The sky is a voice speaking quietly.
Lonely, it drags up the spiders
Into its aching drifting whispers.

The sky is an eye; round, blind,
Milked over without any memory,
Pretending to be alert.

The sky is a pale fingernail;
The cold blue fingertip of an embryo
Stillborn; laid out for the funeral.

Laguna Beach

The shingle roofs burgeon moss, green as tender acacia.
Under their eaves giant roses in cinemascope flash
Over-developed boobs; huge green penises rise, hairy,
Bristling with impotence, into trees that hold them.
Meanwhile the trees wait around on one foot for a place
To set the penises aside. It rains.
The sun draws off all the water.
Nature says yes to everything.

Out of Los Angeles

Coming into St. Louis, our heads still garbled
With Indian Spanish lilt and monotone.
The bus heavy with fumes and bodies.
We ride along the dry grass with herds of black Angus.
Demonic signs advise to gas up, have a Lark,
Get an exciting homesite in Eureka, save bucks on trucks.
Hounding, baying through diseased patches of elms,
Time's mobile sales and Black Madonna Shrine and grotto,
Going America's polluted trail by bus,
Nosing the smell from surf to surf,
Yipping with the dog day after day
On the track of the thief
Who rip-gutted mother earth, our angel mother;
Her belly slit from crotch to Oyster Bay.

The Nose

Everyone complains about the nose.
If you notice, it is stuck to your face.
In the morning it will be red.
If you are a woman you can cover it with makeup.
If you are a man it means you had a good time last night.
Noses are phallic symbols.
So are fingers, monuments, trees, and cucumbers.
The familiar, "He knows his stuff," should be looked into.
There is big business in nose jobs,
The small nose having gained popularity during the Christian
   boom.
Noses get out of joint but a broken nose
Is never the same thing as a broken heart.
They say, "Bless your heart." "Shake hands." "Blow
   your nose."
When kissing there is apt to be a battle of wills
Over which side your nose will go on.
While a nosebleed, next to a good cry, is a natural physic;
A nosey person smells you out and looking down your nose
Will make you cross-eyed.
Although the nose is no longer used for rooting and shoving,
It still gets into some unlikely places.
The old sayings: He won by a nose, and,
He cut off his nose to spite his face,
Illustrate the value of the nose.
In conclusion, three out of four children
Are still equipped with noses at birth;
And the nose, more often than not,
Accompanies the body to its last resting place.

Bazook

My aunt from St. Louis
Lost her husband,
So yesterday I invited her
And Dorothy to lunch.
Over in Dorothy's neighborhood
There was this couple
She used to think so much of —
Fred and Ida.
They had a lovely little house.
For two years all that two talked
Was, wait till we get to Florida,
Wait till we get to Florida.
It's going to be this and that.
Then finally they sold
And moved to Clearwater, Fla.
And built this place.
And the next thing we hear,
The wife's went bazook!
There they were in Clearwater
With this nice little place.
It got so bad Fred finally
Had her committed.
She didn't know him.
He was like a stranger.
He'd go to see her now and again.
But she was like a stranger.
He'd say, "Ida,"
And she wouldn't acknowledge.
He'd say, "It's Fred, Ida."
And the other day
We hear she died.
Now they're coming up to Tuscola
Where she was raised
To have the funeral,
And we're all going over there
To see them.

Something Deeper

I am still at the same subject —
Shredding facts —
As old women nervously
Pull apart
Whatever is put in their fingers;
Undoing all the years
Of mending, putting together;
Taking it apart now
In a stubborn reversal;
Tearing the milky curtain,
After something deeper
That did not occur
In all the time of making
And preparing.

The Song of Absinthe Granny

Among some hills there dwelt in parody
A young woman; me.
I was that gone with child
That before I knew it I had three
And they hung whining and twisting.
Why I wasn't more than thirty-nine
And sparse as a runt fruit tree.
Three pips that plagued the life out of me.
Ah me. It wore me down,
The grubs, the grubbing.
We were two inches thick in dust
For lack of scrubbing.
Diapers and panty-shirts and yolk of eggs.
One day in the mirror I saw my stringy legs
And I looked around
And saw string on the floor,
And string on the chair
And heads like wasps' nests
Full of stringy hair.
"Well," I said, "if you have string, knit.
Knit something, don't just sit."
We had the orchard drops,
But they didn't keep.
The milk came in bottles.
It came until the bottles were that deep
We fell over the bottles.
The milk dried on the floor.
"Drink it up," cried their papa,
And they all began to roar, "More!"
Well, time went on,
Not a bone that wasn't frayed.
Every chit was nicked and bit,
And nothing was paid.
We had the dog spayed.
"It looks like a lifetime,"

Their papa said.
"It's a good life, it's a good wife,
It's a good bed."
So I got the rifle out
To shoot him through the head.
But he went on smiling and sitting
And I looked around for a piece of string
To do some knitting.
Then I picked at the tiling
And the house fell down.
"Now you've done it," he said.
"I'm going to town.
Get them up out of there,
Put them to bed."
"I'm afraid to look," I whimpered,
"They might be dead."
"We're here, mama, under the shed."
Well, the winters wore on.
We had cats that hung around.
When I fed them they scratched.
How the little nippers loved them.
Cats and brats.
I couldn't see for my head was thatched
But they kept coming in when the door unlatched.
"I'll shave my head," I promised,
"I'll clip my mop.
This caterwauling has got to stop."
Well, all that's finished,
It's all been done.
Those were high kick summers,
It was bald galled fun.
Now the daft time's over
And the string is spun.
I'm all alone
To cull and be furry.

Not an extra page in the spanking story.
The wet britches dried
And the teeth came in.
The last one cried
And no new began.
Those were long hot summers,
Now the sun won't tarry.
My birds have flocked,
And I'm old and wary.
I'm old and worn and a cunning sipper,
And I'll outlive every little nipper.
And with what's left I'm chary,
And with what's left I'm chary.

III

from

Topography

Dream of Light in the Shade

Now that I am married I spend
My hours thinking about my husband.
I wind myself about his shelter.
I watch his sleep, dreaming of how to defend
His inert form. At night
Leaning on my elbow I pretend
I am merely a lecherous friend.

And being the first to wake
Often wholly naked descend
To the dim first floor where the chairs
Hold the night before, and all says attend!
The light so coldly spells in innocence,
Attend! The cup is filled with light,
And on my skin the sun flashes
And fades as the shade trees bend.

The Talking Fish

My love's eyes are red as the sargasso
With lights behind the iris like a cephalopod's.
The weeds move slowly, November's diatoms
Stain the soft stagnant belly of the sea.
Mountains, atolls, coral reefs,
Do you desire me? Am I among the jellyfish of your griefs?
I comb my sorrows singing; any doomed sailor can hear
The rising and falling bell and begin to wish
For home. There is no choice among the voices
Of love. Even a carp sings.

Memory of Knowledge and Death
at the Mother of Scholars

Cambridge, England, 1959

Why do we meet at the Backs, you and I,
Bells bumping the wind, swans on the Cam
At Wren's bridge, one-third through March?
Goosed by a deadly hook, a girl's soft body under the ooze;
Let her sleep with the sucked-down refuse.
Our eyes lie on the surface of the water
Like the water flies.
Dons at tea repeat, It is curious and unfortunate,
After the dredging up,
And clasp their hands on their knees.
And the butcher on High Street dies
In a basement among the cans; a wretched suicide.
The gates of the Colleges enameled blue and gold
Swing over worn-away stones.
The swans beat out of the water and rise
Like heralding angels among the trees.
And I send home what's left of you —
Your shoes, your shirts, old theater stubs,
The acrid odor of your sweat in the living dream,
Scholar's paper and lead,
The notes compounded for nothing in the museum.

Being Human

Though all the force to hold the parts together
And service love reversed, turned negative,
Fountained in self-destroying flames
And rained ash in volcanic weather;
We are still here where you left us
With our own kind: unstable strangers
Trembling in the sound waves of meaningless
Eloquence. They say we live.
They say, as they rise on the horizon
And come toward us dividing and dividing,
That we must save; that we must solve; transcend
Cohesive and repelling flesh, protoplasm, particles, and survive.
I do not doubt we will; I do not doubt all things are possible,
Even that wildest hope that we may meet beyond the grave.

Tenacity

Can it be over so soon?
Why, only a day or so ago
You let me win at chess
While you felt my dress
Around the knees.
That room we went to
Sixty miles away —
Have those bus trips ended?
The willows turning by,
Drooping like patient beasts
Under their yellow hair
On the winter fields;
Crossing the snow streams —
Was it for the last time?
Going to meet you, I thought
I saw the embalmer standing there
On the ordinary dirty street
Of that gross and ordinary city
Which opened like a paper flower
At the ballet, at the art gallery,
In those dark booths drinking beer.
One night leaning in a stone doorway
I waited for the wrong person,
And when he came I noticed the dead
Blue color of his skin under the neon light,
And the odor of rubbish behind a subway shed.
I sit for hours at the window
Preparing a letter; you are coming toward me,
We are balanced like dancers in memory,
I feel your coat, I smell your clothes,
Your tobacco; you almost touch me.

The Excuse

Do they write poems when they have something to say,
Something to think about,
Rubbed from the world's hard rubbing in the excess of
    every day?
The summer I was twenty-four in San Francisco. You and I.
The whole summer seemed like a cable-car ride over the
    gold bay.
But once in a bistro, angry at one another,
We quarreled about a taxi fare. I doubt
That it was the fare we quarreled about,
But one excuse is as good as another
In the excess of passion, in the need to be worn away.

Do they know it is cleanness of skin, firmness of flesh that
    matters?
It is so difficult to look at the deprived, or smell their decay.
But now I am among them. I, too, am a leper, a warning.
I hold out my crippled fingers; my voice flatters
Everyone who comes this way. In the weeds of mourning,
Groaning and gnashing, I display
Myself in malodorous comic wrappings and tatters,
In the excess of passion, in the need to be worn away.

Salt

In the bell toll of a clang,
My feet in no snare,
My hand in no hand,
I went to the land of nowhere.

And it came to pass
The live grass spoke to me,
No woman is fair sang the grass,
They eat up the men, sang the grass
And the mist of the hanging tree
Smiled in the beard of Jehovah,
Pass on said the teeth and tongue,
I mean you no harm,
Take care to be strong,
Admit you are wrong.

Farther on by and by
I began to spy
The earth in the eye of a rock,
Then another eye
And another eye,
They ringed me round like a clock.

Weep, was what I thought they implied,
But my eyes were dry as salt.
Nothing would make my tears unlock.
You must pay the penalty, they cried,
If you insist on being a bride
It's all your fault.

And I saw the dark hair roots,
The long arms and the boots
Of despair.
And all the words of the air
Hissed in my ear,

Share!
Take off your flesh and share,
And we'll let you look in
At the sorcerer's virginal house of skin,
Where no woman goes,
For women are nothing but clothes.
And I peeped through the curtain and saw
A houseful of beautiful men.

And then did the boot
And the arm and hair
Come down from the tree
And measure my length with me standing there.
She's too long said the boot,
Too fat said the arm,
The hair sprang to my chin
And my lip like a swarm.
And down with a thud of earth went my form.

In the hourglass
It came to pass
I returned from where I died,
With my funeral veil
And my fairy tale
And the tears I never cried,
And the story's grown stale,
Female and Male,
Where the stars fly,
And we all die
On the down side.

Denouement

You intimidated me. I was thrown into hell without a trial.
Guilty by default. It was clear the murdered one was dead.
There were only two of us. But no one came to lead me away.
A hundred eyes looked in and saw me on fire.
We loved him, they said. Then they forgot.
After many years I knew who it was who had died.
Murderer, I whispered, you tricked me.

Between the Lines

Dear daughter: Well, it's November so it begins to rain.
Taking the dog out for a walk around the Square
Saw Mr. Smythe totter into Sage's for his pear.
He was slashing at the students with his cane.
In the elevator Poochie was out of breath.
She's much too fat; we're all too fat.
Mr. Parker is away on account of a death
But everything's as usual. 45's drain
Backed up in 55's. She was indignant;
Sailed out in peignoir under her muskrat.
The steam pipes smell like mold.
Miss Curant put down yesterday's *Monitor*
To stop the wind from blowing under her door.
My windows tremble with the traffic. It's turning cold.
Mrs. Parker's plants in the basement window need water.
They've been gone five days; they were supposed
To come back yesterday. I stopped in at that spa
And the old man in there pinched me. Enclosed
Is a little check. Call me collect, your ma.

The Plan

I said to myself, do you have a plan?
And the answer was always, no, I have no plan.
Then I would say to myself, you must think of one.
But what happened went on, chaotic with necessary pain.
During the winter the dogs dug moles from their runs
And rolled them blind on the frozen road.
Then the crossbills left at the equinox.
All this time I tried to think of a plan,
Something to bring the points together.
I saw that we move in a circle
But I was wordless in the field.
The smell of green steamed, everything shoved,
But I folded my hands and sat on the rocks.
Here I am, I said, with my eyes.
When they have fallen like marbles from their sockets,
What will become of this? And then I remembered
That there were young moles in my mind's eye,
Whose pink bellies shaded to mauve plush,
Whose little dead snouts sparkled with crystals of frost;
And it came to me, the blind will be leading the blind.

Poles

In the summer under the light ease of laundry fluttering
In the air along with our portion of birds, insects, and lifting
    leaves,
The simple truth is I confine your picture to one room
Where occasionally I go to be struck again by its fierce tragic
    stare.
Summoned to it by a world of trifles, in what I know is a
    mockery
Of despair, it depresses me. Though you cannot condemn or
    pardon
My being one with blood and oxygen, I damn myself
For having eyes and ears and wits, all the time I stand before
    you
Shaking my head at the shame of anything that lies down and
    dies.

Emily

Emily playing on the deck, poplar bending along the rail,
Green sea mountain in troughs of hemlocks,
August ringing the flicker's call;
Who can catch Emily running and laughing
Across the blueberries, over the rocks?
The black-haired golden retriever is roughing,
The apples are turning, the flickers are flying.
Emily runs without sneakers or socks.
Bare and tender as petals of roses,
The feet of the high-born unshod and shocking,
And naked to thorns and splinters and knocks.
And that isn't all—Emily balances on the wall.
What terrible surgery tends to the shrieking;
The treacherous sliver deeply imposes
Its claw like a hawk's, and the heart's blood is crying;
Light as the wind she is down in her tracks.
Always runners and catchers of shadows—
Hawks, shrews, and rabbits, deer mice and owls—
The singing and squeaking and leaping in meadows
Comes to a silence. Immutable rules.
Caught on the thorns of our joys as we run.
Emily, Emily, child of the sun.

Green Apples

In August we carried the old horsehair mattress
To the back porch
And slept with our children in a row.
The wind came up the mountain into the orchard
Telling me something;
Saying something urgent.
I was happy.
The green apples fell on the sloping roof
And rattled down.
The wind was shaking me all night long;
Shaking me in my sleep
Like a definition of love,
Saying, this is the moment,
Here, now.

Haying

Mr. Wanzer is cutting his silage;
His iron cicada sings in the field.
The grasshoppers struggle under the chaff;
Shrews tremble in their hot burrows.
Alas, cry the woodcocks among the alders.
Around and around, to his dump along the brook
Where he husbands the heads of animals
And sacks of oozing offal in the sliding drift.
He shifts his weight; he sweats into his beer.
The grass binds on the tractor wheels
In a crush of green and sweetens to hay;
And a multitude of legs, threshed in the act of begetting,
Shrill into the zenith of the August day.

Habitat

The wolverine, whose numbers remain somewhat constant,
Lays claim to upwards of half a million acres
As his own and his few bitches'.
A relative of the glutton; lonely patriarch;
Restless, cautious and suspicious of man.
(The mammalogist Adolph Murie says
That during his study of the mammals of Mt. Rainier,
He never saw a wolverine.)
He is a shy animal and keeps to outsized, secret paths.
He is the largest of the mustelines —
That subfamily which claims the mink, the weasel.
Dr. Krott is amazed at the uniformity of the species,
Which is of circumpolar distribution,
Inhabiting the vast coniferous forests of the north.
The quality of the pelts in Manchuria, however,
Is said to be slightly inferior.
Man has driven him from the southern fringes
Of Latvia, Estonia, and some Russian provinces.
His body averages three feet long including the tail.
His weight is sometimes nearly eighty pounds.
He is built for endurance;
Indeed, it is said that lumbosacrally he is overbuilt.
When engaged with a wolf in the powdery snow of the
    wooded area,
The wolverine happily proves to be superior.
Since man has rid himself of the plague of wolves,
The wolverine is moving into the tundra.
He is an animal fond of play and can learn something new
To his innate modes of behavior. When caught in a trap
He may bite off the tortured limb and escape.
He runs in serpentine lines with frequent change of direction.
Strong hunger keeps a wolverine awake.
In the winter he is the scourge of the Laplanders' reindeer.
His normal gait is the gallop, and when pursued
He can cover forty miles without a rest.

Though carnivorous, he decimates at the proper season
The larvae of wasps. He is a voracious rampant eater of
   wasp larvae,
Digging them out in the singing buzz and sting
From their mud-packed niches.
He has a fur much valued by northern peoples,
Which does not mat; men wear it about their faces.
He marks off his half-million acres with his own urine,
And each of his bitches knows her own parcel
By the singular smell of her feces.

Eclat

Mrs. Tory shaves her boarders' whiskers
When they come home from Brighton
In the high seats of their empty lorries.
But who cut her old man's beard?
It was flourishing when he ate the poached morels
At the kitchen table, leaning on his elbows
And clicking his cutlery in the juice.
While she stropped her razor
He was telling her whose pig rooted up High Street.
But who cut the old man's beard?

The beard of the old man
Was stolen in his own kitchen by Mrs. Tory.
She dropped the hairs behind the stove,
And put her whetstone on the shelf of the pantry
By the dish of butter.
And when he woke naked to his own hands,
He trembled, thinking he was in his bridal bed,
With all those years ahead of him.
But he never let it be known.
He called out the same as every day,
"Mrs. Tory, fetch me my tea."

The Principle of Mirrors

The wind turns a windmill in Australia
Clattering like a loose tin roof.
This sort of thing is accessible;
You simply put your arm through the TV
And pick up the little people
Who are climbing the windmill
In order to fix it.
They are really only lizards.
It's very different
The way the same creatures,
Perhaps not quite the same creatures,
Stretch out, swing around and revolve,
Sliding away in stock pens cunningly designed
With no turning back;
Hooting and hollering in Texas
On a ribbon of smoke.
Cattle accompany you without moving from their positions
In the shade of yucca.
Consider the stationary expansion
Of a plain percale sheet
Holding the mattress in place,
Upon which the mass of entrails,
Suspended in fluid, contracts and writhes
While the entire thing vibrates
With systolic knocks.
(The noise is that of a body in need of repair.)
It has gone to bed to ingest
Gin and tonic, rare steak, baked potatoes,
Sour cream, tossed salad.
Poor Bill, everyone sighs;
If only they would vary the flight pattern.
The real vision comes in walls of glass.
A man with a square red beard approaches.
"Tell them," he says, as he slowly floats by,
"Hello for me."
If you would take the trouble to examine skulls

You would find that the fixed smile
Is a partial spasm of facial muscles
And that the jaw is hinged rather nicely
For a variety of functions,
Primarily rending and chewing.
Here, picking up black scorpions
Imbedded in plastic,
It clearly says,
"Poisonous."
You have to understand
I'm writing this
As though I'm running.
It's done
With very little breath.
"Good-bye" (we are
Exaggerating with our lips
While we shed our skin),
I declare it's too bad,
I have left you my dead hand!
Put it in the disposal
If yours is the kind
That will take bones.
Now let's not say that word,
Shall we?
Somewhere in Chicago
I pull out a cactus spine.
"So that's what I was sitting on,"
I say to the lady in the good silk suit
Who has taken off her shoes
And exposed the most horrendous bunion.
"Folks" — the conductor oozes up the aisle,
Swaying suspiciously —
"Get out your Bibles.
We are all going to pray as we pull into the station."
"Nonsense!" I shout.
"You're nothing but a pack of words."

Behind the Façade

My mother stayed in her small room
With the door not quite shut.
We watched TV in the living room,
Walter and I;
Secure,
Our arms lightly touching.
We couldn't remember
That my father had died.
Mother lay quietly
Staring into no language,
No touch,
The emptiness of nothing
Which had been there all the time
Behind the façade.
On the couch, with our backs to her door,
We leaned together
Talking about the children;
Our friends, the Late Late Show.
We felt our way among words
As on steel girders;
The structure multicolored, real.
Objects lay all around
Shaping the air.
Concrete as the glass of beer,
The cutlery;
Our arms holding one another;
Binding together what we said . . .
What we said . . . what we said.

I Have Three Daughters

I have three daughters
Like greengage plums.
They sat all day
Sucking their thumbs.
And more's the pity,
They cried all day,
Why doesn't our mother's brown hair
Turn gray?

I have three daughters
Like three cherries.
They sat at the window
The boys to please.
And they couldn't wait
For their mother to grow old.
Why doesn't our mother's brown hair
Turn to snow?

I have three daughters
In the apple tree
Singing Mama send Daddy
With three young lovers
To take them away from me.

I have three daughters
Like greengage plums,
Sitting all day
And sighing all day
And sucking their thumbs;
Singing, Mama won't you fetch and carry,
And Daddy, won't you let us marry,
Singing, sprinkle snow down on Mama's hair
And lordy, give us our share.

A Mother Looks at Her Child

Why are you beautiful?
Was it your mother, your father,
Your genes?
I don't understand you.
Was it your aunts, your uncles?
I think of your unborn sisters and brothers,
Circuitous protein.
Who are they,
Lost in the serpent and the scale,
Who might have been?
Infinitely small
Ovoid, tail.
Why are you beautiful?

I am flesh set seal.
The other all.
Splitting skeins,
Roof, periphery, hall,
Doorway on the finite.
Why are you beautiful?

Are these the only eyes in which you flash
And flare in the burning blood?
There in the center, misunderstood
Great ornamental tree;
Limbs, sinewy arms, interlocking hair,
Igniting the air.
Separate flash whose fall cannot fail.
Why are you beautiful?

Advice

My hazard wouldn't be yours, not ever;
But every doom, like a hazelnut, comes down
To its own worm. So I am rocking here
Like any granny with her apron over her head
Saying, lordy me. It's my trouble.
There's nothing to be learned this way.
If I heard a girl crying help
I would go to save her;
But you hardly ever hear those words.
Dear children, you must try to say
Something when you are in need.
Don't confuse hunger with greed;
And don't wait until you are dead.

End of Summer . . . 1969

Dear Phoebe, wherever you are,
The old maple on the brook, the one scarred by lightning,
Has tipped me the warning . . . summer's gone.
Dear Marcia, the faces of mutilated girls
Lie on the streets of Ann Arbor.
Whose face is dear to me? O world, O galaxy,
My error is to look for meaning in the sun
That burns for burning. I love you, apple tree.

Dear Abigail, the last severe and structured answer to my soul,
My arms are useless. In the dark ovoid chamber
What I clasped was God, who could not reveal
To the grass, to the grains of sand,
Or remember that what he dreamed was real.

Dear Mother, and sisters and brothers, dear nieces,
All at once proclaim in a loud voice
Summer is over. In the traces
Of broken stars it is too late for truces and wars.
You must go down the long stairway
Into the dark coal sack of the sky;
O love, O longing, O world that was before.

Seat Belt Fastened?

Old Bill Pheasant won't trim his beard.
Weep, my daughters, and have you heard?
Sing, little otters; don't be afraid.
There's a rustle in the oak leaves
Down by the river. Oh, the moving mirror
And the hearer and the word.

Old Bill wandered in my waking dream,
A river dream; when I saw him come
I was riding by with my gas tank high
Down to Otter Creek from my just-right home.
And he put his beard in the window and said,
"It's sleazy and greasy but it's in your head.
Tell me woman, do you carry a comb?"
Too far from home to the river, I shammed.
"Better not come this far," I said.
But old Bill Pheasant said he'd be damned.
And we backfired down. Oh, daughers, do you tread
On the leaf fall, fern all—picked and pocketed?

Now tell me when we're passing, and tell me when we gain.
And laugh, little children, while our gas tank's high.
"Give thanks for desire," was all he said.
"It'll either clear up or snow or rain."
So we tweaked his beard and we punched his head.
Is your seat belt fastened? Do you sleep in your bed?
If you're stuck in the river can you shift to red?
If you're coming are you going?
If you're living are you dead?

And we drove him away where the otters play,
Where it's twice on Sunday in the regular way,
Where they say what they know and they know what they say,
And the good time's coming on yesterday.

Disappeared Child

If only I could wrest you out of nothing,
Muscle and fat, with every hair intact,
And give you back this painful air we breathe.

Or else I ought not to have conceived,
Wrapped in those sinews I was taught to love,
Nailed by a martyred madman.

To let you go this way, naïve and terrible
Into the scream of silence in my head!
You are not there. . . . Nor were you ever there.

Every move to contemplate the passing of cell to cell—
Which girdled round, becomes in your flesh
The woman measured into the child—

Is blind seeing; calling to the blind,
To find that which was not; was inward;
The light of darkness which lies everywhere.

The Story of the Churn

I am so rich and poor, cried the widow;
My children are scattered.
When storms come up
And cast the dark shadow,
And tongues of the lightning flicker,
I hide in the root cellar.

And the turnip mutters to me,
What princess is guttering here?
The onions leach their smell;
The potatoes turn on their sides and leer.
I am so rich and poor,
I watch the sky through a slit in the door.

Out in the sty the pig waits for his slop;
In circles of prickly flesh
He looks me in the eye and turns away;
I have hired a young man for the rutabaga crop.

Who is this princess stuttering here?
Murmurs the cabbage; by what quorum
Does she cower here out of the storm
When she lives above the stair?
Let us put spiders in her hair.

I am so rich and poor. My buckets are full
Of milk, and my pantry wheezes
With rancid butter and heavy cheeses.
I have no fat little faces
To dip their lips in the chips
And swipe the greases.
Oh, thin, thin, thin like a tailor's pin
I slide in the cracks of my pantry wall;
There are no children here at all.
The food spills into the cellar like gall.

I look at the seeds who are fierce
And swell with impatience; they sneer at the weeds
In the vegetable patch. And the eggs in the hen house
Knock in their shells and hatch.
I am so rich; no one else has a roof like mine
With a fine design in the thatch.

If only the lightning would strike
And suck up the working casks of beer,
Turnips and cabbages, onions and cheeses;
And burn up the quilts, the cribs, and laces;
And sweep my fields dry, where the delicate faces
Of all the children in their hiding places
Creep away from me now in the fire and shadow.
Oh, I am so rich and so poor, cried the widow.

It

Oh the pretty tinsel of it,
the wind-blown glass chimes of it.
The leaf-colored flower-strewn
wandering way of it.
Oh the rain of it, the gray-hewn day of it,
the ballooning thunder of it,
the warbling throats and the
plaintive songs of it.
The catarrh and the complaining of it.
The blunder of it;
the goats and the asses of it;
the ghastly wrongs of it.
The insidious hunger of it,
the giving and the taking
and the languor of it.
The eating of flesh
and the rejecting of it.
The doubling and the tripling
and the quadrupling of it.
And the sun and the sunlight
and the terrible sustaining of it.

Metamorphosis

Now I am old, all I want to do is try;
But when I was young, if it wasn't easy I let it lie,
Learning through my pores instead,
And it did neither of us any good.

For now she is gone who slept away my life,
And I am ignorant who inherited,
Though the head has grown so lively that I laugh,
"Come look, come stomp, come listen to the drum."

I see more now than then; but she who had my eyes
Closed them in happiness, and wrapped the dark
In her arms and stole my life away,
Singing in dreams of what was sure to come.

I see it perfectly, except the beast
Fumbles and falters, until the others wince.
Everything shimmers and glitters and shakes with unbearable
    longing,
The dancers who cannot sleep, and the sleepers who cannot
    dance.

Topography

Do I dare to think that I alone am
The sum total of every night hand searching in the
Pounding pounding over the universe of veins, sweat,
Dust in the sheets with noses that got in the way?
Yes, I remember the turning and holding,
The heavy geography; but map me again, Columbus.

IV

from

In an Iridescent Time

The Magnet

I loved my lord, my black-haired lord, my young love
Thin faced, pointed like a fox,
And he, singing and sighing, with the bawdy went crying
Up the hounds, through thicket he leaped, through bramble,
And crossed the river on rocks.
And there alongside the sheep and among the ewes and lambs,
With terrible sleep he cunningly laid his hoax.

Ah fey, and ill-gotten, and wicked his tender heart,
Even as they with their bahs and their niggles, rumped up the
    thistle and bit
With their delicate teeth the flowers and the seeds and the leaf,
He leaped with a cry as coarse as the herders, "Come, I will
    start,

Come now my pretties, and dance, to the hunting horn and the
  slit
Of your throbbing throats, and make me a coat out of grief."
And they danced, he was fey, and they danced, and the coat
  they made
Turned all of an innocent mind, and a single love, into
  beasts afraid.

Was it I called him back? was it hunger? was it the world?
Not my tears, not those cries of the murdered, but 'twas the
  fox
Hid in the woods who called, and the smell of the fox, burned
  in his mind,
The fox in his den, smiling, around his red body his fine plume
  curled,
Out of the valley and across the river, leaving his sheep's
  hair, he left the maligned flocks,
I heard him coming through brambles, through narrow forests,
  I bid my nights unwind,
I bid my days turn back, I broke my windows, I unsealed my
  locks.

In an Iridescent Time

My mother, when young, scrubbed laundry in a tub,
She and her sisters on an old brick walk
Under the apple trees, sweet rub-a-dub.
The bees came round their heads, the wrens made talk.
Four young ladies each with a rainbow board
Honed their knuckles, wrung their wrists to red,
Tossed back their braids and wiped their aprons wet.
The Jersey calf beyond the back fence roared;
And all the soft day, swarms about their pet
Buzzed at his big brown eyes and bullish head.
Four times they rinsed, they said. Some things they starched,
Then shook them from the baskets two by two,
And pinned the fluttering intimacies of life
Between the lilac bushes and the yew:
Brown gingham, pink, and skirts of Alice blue.

The Season

I know what calls the Devil from the pits,
With a thief's fingers there he slouches and sits;
I've seen him passing on a frenzied mare,
Bitter eyed on her haunches out to stare;
He rides her cruel and he rides her easy.
Come along spring, come along sun, come along field daisy.

Smell the foxy babies, smell the hunting dog;
The shes have whelped, the cocks and hens have lost their wits;
And cry, "Why," cry the spring peepers, "Why," each little
    frog.
He rides her cruel and he rides her easy;
Come along spring, come along sun, come along field daisy.

The Burned Bridge

Sister was wedged beside the wicker basket,
Slats of hot midsummer striped her dress,
Speckled dust in shifting sun and shadow.
The trolley lurched to leeward, seemed to press
Our bodies backward in a flowered meadow,
Tossed mama's brown hair sculptured in a puff.
Father rose and reeling from our side
Interviewed the trenchant motorman. How rough
The whitecaps glittered beyond the marsh;
Our pulses leaped at the stench of kelp and the harsh
Scream of the cormorant skimming the trolley wire.
Halfway on the clanging headlong ride
The trolley crossed a bridge charred black from fire
And reason impaled me, even through mama's smile
And the arc of the motorman's tobacco juice.
"There, there," soothed mama; "The deuce!" said father.
But knowing better, I cried.
Though we went on for mile after summer mile
And arrived as we always did at the rank seaside,
All that held me up seemed wholly mad.
Not even the hidden drop-off, or bloated death
In the luminous choppy water, diverted my sad
Foreboding, or the derelict lighthouse in whose shade we
    lunched.
At sunset sister slept like a rosy anchor
Fastening parents to bench, and while they bunched
The tide rolled softly landward like her breath;
While I sat listening, wretched, without rancor,
Submissive on the bench beside the track.
Knowing, this time, the burned bridge would break,
I clearly saw my parents committed to folly.
Mama, for all her airs, could but clean and bake.
Now father, as in a nightmare, would take us back;
And hooting around the bend came the feckless trolley.

Orchard

The mare roamed soft about the slope,
Her rump was like a dancing girl's.
Gentle beneath the apple trees
She pulled the grass and shook the flies.
Her forelocks hung in tawny curls;
She had a woman's limpid eyes,
A woman's patient stare that grieves.
And when she moved among the trees,
The dappled trees, her look was shy,
She hid her nakedness in leaves.
A delicate though weighted dance
She stepped while flocks of finches flew
From tree to tree and shot the leaves
With songs of golden twittering;
How admirable her tender stance.
And then the apple trees were new,
And she was new, and we were new,
And in the barns the stallions stamped
And shook the hills with trumpeting.

The Splinter

I had a little silver manikin
Who walked and talked and petted me;
I pampered him, he pampered me; we
Were convivial. On the gray streets
Of many a gray city he wept with me.
Oh then how miniature was sin,
How clear its purpose like a looking glass
To show me my young girl's skin.

But I looked and looked again
And saw a blue cadaverous vein.
I will grow old, I cried,
You are a silver groom,
I will be a brown leather bride.
You are imperishable, still by my side
You will shine in the wine
That puckers my hide.

And in these sad reflections
I took a silver hammer made of words,
And hit him and he shattered like bright birds
Flying in all directions.
All night and all eternity I cried,
And in the morning by the gray light
I found his splinter in my side,
And when I drew it out, I saw it was glass —
The finest concave mirror, silver white
And backed with brightest silver. Oh alas,
He was a manikin of glass with all his light turned in,
And mirrored in the dark, the manikin.

The Mold

As you swing the door your passage through air
Sends back the pale vibration of your disapproval
And crossly shakes the curtain, puffs the fire to flare,
And settles like coal dust, which though we remove all
Signs of it with cloth and wax is still there.

I would be with you on the ill-carpeted stairs
Climbing toward your unheated room in stretching pain,
That all-elastic anguish of the child. You think, who cares?
And following your tragic side up to the laceration of your
    prayers,
I recall the single beds where I have lain.

In this bruising of spirits and this pulling of feathers
From angel's wings we reduce you to clay,
For that is how we are made. That airy flight in all weathers
Subsides, until well formed, we drag from our beds toward day.

An Old Song

When I was young I knew that I would die.
The fear of an old death went out with me.
The rank green wasted; fiddle, so did I,
But I was long-lived as the hemlock tree.

Yes, I was strong as juniper. The pitch,
The amber resin, all of those strong tars,
The pungent aromatics of the bitch,
I kept in fascinating rows of jars.

All those other odors. Love's a smell.
I'll dance the diddy on a wrinkled knee;
The empty udders dangle on the shell.
Now the fat's gone, some gnaw the bone with me.

I tell you death's hard fought for, hard to kill.
On powdered mirrors these death's eyes outstare
The old bold adversary of the will.
I am the death, and who comes for his share?

Love's Relative

The couple who remain in bed
Are not alike; he's tanned and hairy,
Has a fierce Egyptian head,
She's dimpled, brief; alas, contrary.

Rather defenseless on the sheet
When morning oozes in the cracks,
Her tiny toes, his monster feet,
Both of them upon their backs.

Her years are two and his are thirty.
He's long and bony, somewhat glum.
Her little peaceful feet are dirty.
She sucks a firmly calloused thumb.

At some point in the evil dawning
This oedipal arrangement grew,
The leap from crib to bed while yawning
Mother in disdain withdrew.

O man, whose waking breeds confusion,
Protect the comfort of her sleep,
Hers is the primal bright illusion
From which she makes the bridal leap.

Vernal Equinox

Daughters, in the wind's boisterous roughing,
Pray the tickle's equal to the coat tearing,
And the wearing equal to the puffing,
As you match breath and tugging after the winter
In the thaw and the first heat of the sun's splinter.

In your first ramble, daughters, with your laughing
Loosed from the freeze when the grass is seeping,
Save your dimpled knees in the headstrong leaping.

And under his cloak, if you run with the north wind
When there is the smell of hibernation in him
And the black half-frozen waters of a dam,
Watch for his cruelty, he traps the lamb.

Daughters under the birches in the green weeping,
In the rain and lightning of the west wind's keeping,
Daughters, does, with tawny flanks shy stamping,
Nibble his water-quick land with your hoofs tamping,
And dance, do not rest, or he'll have you sleeping.

And daughters whose hearts are going
Higher, higher with your wild hair blowing
Into his high-riding giant's bellows,
Observe the tremble of the weeping willows.

About the Author

Ruth Stone has been a Guggenheim Fellow and a member of the Radcliffe Institute. Her work has appeared in *The New Yorker* and literary magazines everywhere. She has taught at Indiana, Illinois, Wisconsin, Brandeis, and New York universities and has read at the YM and YWHA Poetry Center in New York City. She received the Delmore Schwartz Award for Poetry (1984) and, in 1986, one of the second annual Whiting Writers' Awards.